LET MY BABIES GO!
A Passover Story

Based on the TV series *Rugrats*® created by Klasky/Csupo Inc. and Paul Germain as seen on Nickelodeon®

SIMON SPOTLIGHT
An imprint of Simon & Schuster
Children's Publishing Division
1230 Avenue of the Americas
New York, New York 10020

Manufactured in the United States of America

First Edition   10 9 8 7 6 5 4 3 2

ISBN 0-689-81979-X

LET MY BABIES GO!
A Passover Story

By Sarah Willson

From the script by Peter Gaffney, Paul Germain,
Jonathan Greenberg, and Rachel Lipman

Illustrations by Barry Goldberg

Simon Spotlight/Nickelodeon

"What kind of dumb holiday is this?" snorted Angelica. She and Tommy and Chuckie were visiting Tommy's grandparents for Passover. "No cookies, no presents, not even any toys to play with!"

"Passover, dumb?" cried Grandpa Boris. "Passover is a time for Jewish families to share the history of their people! Gather round, *kinderlach*, and I will tell you the story. Imagine you were there!" And he began . . .

Thousands of years ago, a people called the Egyptians built great cities. Their leader, Pharaoh, decided that the Hebrew people would be slaves. The slaves were forced to move heavy stones and to work in the hot sun.

But it was soon foretold that a boy leader of the Hebrew people would one day overthrow Pharaoh. Pharaoh became afraid and decided to get rid of all the boy babies.

One Hebrew slave wanted to save her baby. So she put him in a little boat and sent him down the river.

It wasn't long before Pharaoh spotted the little baby from the royal barge.

"Hiya!" cried Pharaoh. "Where you from?"

"Uh, up the river, I guess," said the baby, whose name was Moses.

Pharaoh invited Moses to come back to the palace. Of course, Pharaoh did not know that Moses was a Hebrew.

Pharaoh showed Moses around. Moses was very impressed with the lovely palace and the large buildings. But he also noticed some slaves who were working very hard.

One day, Moses went up to the slaves. "Hey!" he called to them. "Why are you all working so hard when you could be playing instead?"

The Hebrew babies looked at one another. "Pharaoh says all Hebrew babies must be slaves!" they said to Moses.

"But I'm a Hebrew baby too!" cried Moses. The slave babies gasped.

The Egyptians were angry when they found out that Moses was a Hebrew baby.
They chased him away and he ran far into the desert.

Living in the desert, Moses forgot all about Egypt and Pharaoh and the Hebrew slaves. Then one day, a burning bush spoke to him. It told him to return to Egypt.

Moses returned to Pharaoh's palace. He stood before Pharaoh and cried, "Let my babies go!"

"No way," Pharaoh replied. "Why should I listen to a little Hebrew baby?"

"You better," said Moses, "or I will let loose some plagues."

Pharaoh just laughed and called to the guards to throw him out. But Moses didn't care. He let loose the plagues.

First he sent the plague of frogs . . .

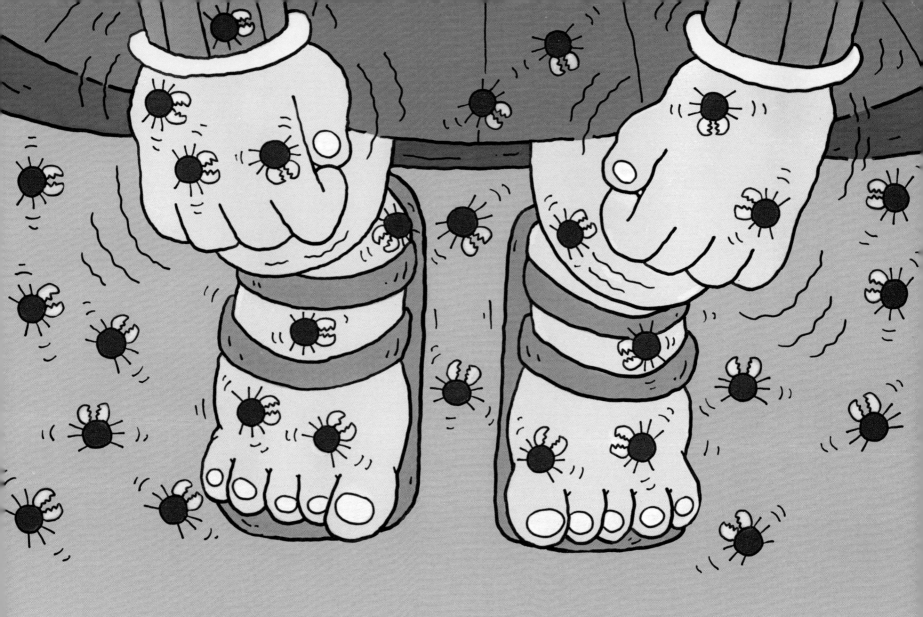

then the plague of lice . . .

then the plague of darkness . . .

then the plague of locusts . . .

and then the plague of wild beasts.

"Okay, okay! Call off your plagues!" cried Pharaoh. "I hereby decree that you babies can go free."

"Hooray!" shouted the babies.

Just as the Hebrew babies were about to leave Egypt, Pharaoh said, "I changed my mind. You gotta stay after all."

Moses got angry. "That's not fair, Pharaoh!" he cried. "Since you didn't keep your promise, I'm gonna rain down the worst plague ever! Tonight the plague is gonna come take away all the firstborn babies!"

"Psst! What about us?" whispered a Hebrew baby to Moses.

"Don't worry," Moses whispered back. "We'll have a red mark on our door, which will tell the plague to pass over our homes. That's why this holiday is gonna be called 'Passover.'"

Finally the Egyptians realized Moses meant business.
"Okay! I changed my royal mind again!" said Pharaoh. "Just
call off all these plagues and get outta here!"

The Hebrew babies left so fast, they had to bring flat
bread without any yeast in it. "We'll call this 'matzo,'" they said.

But once more, Pharaoh decided that the Hebrew babies should not be set free. Pharaoh's army chased the babies all the way to the Red Sea.

"Now what do we do?" the babies wailed, as they looked to Moses for help. The sea was in front of them. Pharaoh's army was behind them. They had *nowhere* to run!

Moses looked up at the heavens and then at the sea. Lo and behold, the waters of the sea parted! The Hebrew babies cheered and ran between the waves to the other side.

Pharaoh's army came after them, but the waters joined together again, and the soldiers had to quickly swim back. Moses and his people were very happy—they were finally free!

"So every year we have a seder, a ceremony that celebrates how Moses led the Hebrews out of Egypt to freedom!" Grandpa Boris said, as he looked around. "You liked the story of Passover, *kinderlach*?"

Tommy and Chuckie smiled at Grandpa Boris.

"Hold on!" said Angelica. "You call this a reason to celebrate? What about poor Pharaoh, who had no more babies to boss around? And what about all those lice and frogs and stuff? How'd Pharaoh get them out of the palace? If you ask me—"

Just then, Grandma Minka came in, carrying a tray. "Here, *kinderlach*, some Passover treats for all you good babies," she said.

"Hmm . . . " said Angelica, as she popped a treat into her mouth. "Like I was saying, if you ask me, Passover is a *very* cool holiday!"